THE UNEXPECTED

SHREYA S

Contents

Dedicated To

Everyone who is hanging to a dying thread of hope!

Acknowledgements

I thank everyone who has helped me to write this book.

Acknowledgements

Prologue

I never thought this might happen someday

Now I am just wondering about how my life is gonna be now. Now everything seems to be ending, now that everything seems to be gone, now that everything's so messed up. I don't know how long it has been since I left this place, the window of my bedroom. It has always been my hanging spot for my entire life. I used to come here because it made me who I am, it was my happy place but to my surprise, I haven't been myself lately. Even when all I do is sit here. I have not read a book not even a single quote, I haven't eaten since I don't know when I haven't talked to anyone, I haven't seen anyone for a while now not even my family, I haven't showered nor have I brushed my teeth. I haven't heard anything other than the stillness in the room and sometimes people banging on the door as if they were trying to break inside, but no one ever dared to do so as if they knew what they would see. See me in this broken state, broken is underestimating what I felt. It is more than that. I never thought my heart could be this damaged, I never thought I would be this hurt, this broken that I can no longer feel anything left inside me. In the mornings or the afternoons I could feel my blood vessels burning up my whole body, in the chilly nights or evenings I could feel my body freezing up but despite all this, it couldn't move me, not even by an inch. Sometimes I use to feel the rain droplets on my face as if nature wanted me to cry, wanted me to show it that I wasn't dead. I haven't cried since that day. I just couldn't. I felt the pain but no tears could justify how bad it was. After many hours, days or weeks the pain faded away but left me with emptiness. Maybe it left me because I was too used to it, maybe because I was too comfortable with it, maybe because I started being okay with it. The emptiness was surprisingly more disturbing and weakening than the pain I had felt earlier. At first, I lived with misery but now I am the misery. I never felt this empty. It's not like I haven't felt pain or emptiness, I have! I survived depression, anxiety, loneliness and whatnot. I fought it all and it has made me nothing but stronger. I never thought anything could break me again. I thought I was so broken that nothing could ever break me again but I guess I was wrong, perhaps I was always wrong. I never knew losing someone could affect you this much. I never thought losing her would affect me this much. Everything is a blur since that day I don't know how many days have passed by. I was so shocked by this news I just couldn't handle it. I wish things could have been different for us. I wish I could have been a little more careful about things, a little more of myself. I wish I wouldn't have been so foolish, I wish I could have saved you from my thoughts, from myself. I wish I could go back in time and trust you a little more, maybe you would still be by my side. I should have trusted you a little more, maybe I wouldn't have lost you today. Maybe you could have fixed me someday. You were my last hope, my last wish and maybe my last love and I lost you. ***I lost you. Maybe I was never meant to be fixed!***

ONE

The Beginning

"I still cannot believe how we became friends. No one will believe us if we tell them our story, don't you think so Aarohi?" said Myra, staring at me.

"Sure people would believe this, they have to believe it. When you could believe in me even when I am such a weirdo and I don't know crazy? Yeah, that's the word for it. Crazy! Then why not our story? It is the same weird crazy but moreover, it is an epic one. The kind you don't easily find but when you do it lasts forever." I said, staring back at her.

"Well you sure are right about this but I don't think your first book would be about me am I right? I hope you know what I mean." Myra said as she giggled.

"Oh shut up Myra he is just a known stranger. Why on earth would I write a book about him? Vihaan is a good human and I think we have become good friends now. so now I will finally have a friend other than you." I said looking straight at her eyes with a smirk on my face.

"Oh so now you need friends huh? I am no longer enough for you or what?" Myra said, making a puppy face.

"Yeah, you know I get bored of you too, just like aunt," I said, continuing with a laugh.

"DO NOT SAY I AM OVERREACTING BECAUSE I AM NOT. Ahh! Oh my god oh my god, Arohi found a friend, oh what fun it will be to make Arohi blush all day yay, oh my god, oh my god Arohi found a friend!" Myra said laughing

"Oh my God Myra! Stop it, you are insane. And now go get your ass dressed because we are going out to grab a bite and then go shopping." I said, giving her the eye.

"What the. Wait, what did you just say?" Myra said, making a face.

"WE ARE GOING OUT TO GRAB A BITE AND THEN GO SHOPPING" I shouted back at her as I walked towards the bathroom.

"Out? For a bite? And shopping? Since when did you wanna do such things? If this was a prank I swear I will kill you" Mrya said in a very surprised tone.

"OH MY GOD Myra! Just chill, okay this is not a prank. I seriously wish to go out and buy myself some new clothes. Maybe." I said as I made a face at her.

"You are freaking me out, I am calling mom! MA if you are there come here right now! MA" Myra screamed at the top of her lungs.

"Myra!!! What happened? Is Arohi okay? Are you okay?" Aunt said as she came upstairs rushing towards our room.

"Yes, Aunt I am fine Myra is overreacting over stupid things again. I think we should get her checked too, maybe she is even crazier than me." I said with a smile.

"Oh, you two will kill me someday. Myra please never do this again. I was so worried but I am glad you both are fine. Let me know if you need anything but don't scream." said aunt in a very annoyed tone.

"So Arohi what you wanna do now that you have given me and mom a heart attack?" said Myra with her eyebrows raised.

"Oh, so it was all me right? You did nothing right? You never do anything right?" I said looking straight into her eyes.

"Okay, I am sorry but can we go shopping now? I am dying to see you shop for yourself. I am gonna go get dressed." Myra said with the biggest smile on her face.

"Yeah, I am a bit nervous though and I wanna get something fancy but not too fancy you know?" I said nervously.

"I don't understand one thing though why do you want to buy something "fancy and not too fancy" all of a sudden that too by your choice?" Myra asked.

"Ummm please don't scream okay? I am gonna go meet Vihaan so I just wanna look like a normal girl?" I said, staring blankly at Myra waiting for her to scream.

"OHHHH MYYYY OHHHH MYYYY GOD! What did you just say? What did you say?" Myra Screamed.

"What is it now, Myra? Shut up otherwise the neighbours are gonna make us move from here. Arohi stuffed her mouth with something. This girl is such a headache sometimes." aunt shouted from the kitchen.

"MA Aarohi, our Arohi made a new friend and wants to go shopping to buy herself clothes because she is meeting her friend, can you believe this MA?" screamed Myra.

"Myra doesn't shout, I don't want everyone in our neighbourhood to know that." I shot at Myra. "Aunt, it's not that big a deal, is it?" I asked my aunt for reassurance.

"Arohi what are you gonna get yourself? Do you have anything specific in your mind?" Aunt asked me.

"MA, that's what you ask her?" Myra asked aunt in shock.

"I am looking for something fancy but not so fancy," I answered. "She is just not surprised Myra, she kinda knows about this already. I told her about this yesterday." I said, looking at Myra hoping she wouldn't explode.

"WHAT! Why does she know it before I do?" Myra said with an angry face.

"Because you sleep a lot. And miss the gossips, sleepyhead. And of course, she knew, why else do you think she didn't rush to our room when you shouted?" I said as I giggled.

"Huh, that's not fair. That's so not fair." Myra fussed. "Okay well, let's just get going. We are leaving now and maa let me handle this. We three can go out sometime later now that she is meeting her new friend, he is gonna change her. I don't think she will hang out with me after that." Myra said as she giggled.

"Oh shut up Myra! Let's just go." I said as I smiled.

"Oh my god, oh my god, Arohi found a friend, oh what fun it is to make Arohi blush all day yay, oh my god oh my god, Arohi found a friend." Myra sang as she giggled.

"Arohi, I think we really should get this cracked head checked," Aunt said, smiling.

"Yeah, we really should. She is even crazier than me." I said laughing as we went downstairs.

We bid goodbye to Aunt and left the house. Myra was very excited but I was not so much. I am nervous about meeting him and I don't know if I will ever find a dress I like that looks good. I really wanna look presentable at least. We are meeting after a long time.

TWO

The Perfect Dress

So we went to eat. The food part was done nicely. Now comes the hardest part choosing a perfect dress for me. After me talking and Myra screaming for like half an hour, we headed to the mall. After browsing for like 15 to 20 minutes which seemed like forever to me, we choose a bunch of clothes and she made me try them all and then had her screaming session after every one of them and as you may know by now that went on for a while.

One of them was a white gorgeous floral dress and when I came out of the dressing room Myra shouted

“Oh my god Arohi. You look like a girl. That too not just any girl but a gorgeous one. I am telling you he is not gonna stop staring at you”

“OH my god Myra stop shouting everyone is looking at us, this is so embarrassing,” I said nervously.

“I can’t help it, it’s your first date. How can I not be excited?” Myra shouted with excitement.

“Oh no no it’s not a date Myra. It’s just two people meeting for brunch, a cup of coffee and having a conversation." I said as I gave her the eye.

"Yeah sure. If it's not a date then why are you trying so hard to look good huh?" said Myra smiling at me like a child.

"Because I would like to make a good impression and I am so tired of you always shouting. I deserve a normal friend don't you think?" I said as I shut the door to try on the next dress.

"New friend you say," Myra said.

There was a Kurta-like dress in yellow colour with flowers printed on it. I was kinda surprised Myra choose this.

"So Myra, how do I look?" I asked Myra.

"WOW, Aarohi it's so good to see you like this. My girly girl. My girl is finally growing up. But this isn't the best choice for a date, don't you think so?" Myra said, smiling.

"Oh, Myra, stop it. It's not a date. I am just gonna go try the next dress." I said, giving her an angry look.

There was a polka dot flare dress that was my favourite so far.

"Here, how do I look? I like this one Myra." I said smiling.

"PERFECT! Hot and cute at the same time. If this isn't a date then he is gonna ask you out today." said Myra, giving me a smirk.

"Just friends. Myra. Okay, I am really tired now. Can we just buy this one please and get the hell out of here?" I said with an annoyed look on my face.

"Umm okay but just try on the last one. Please for me." Myra begged.

It was a black bodycon dress with white stripes on its sides.

"Umm okay. How do I look?" I asked uncertainly.

“YOU IDIOT. YOU LOOK HOT AF AAROHI. I never knew you were blessed with such a great body. Why would someone wear sweatpants and loose tops if that person has such a great figure like you?” screamed Myra in shock. “If you wear this you are not gonna come home tomorrow night” Myra teased me.

“Myra firstly keep your voice down please and how many times do I have to tell you this isn’t a date, nothing is gonna happen between us okay?” I said angrily.

“Fine, Aarohi but whose voice is high now?” Myra said, giving me the eye.

“Please can we skip this and just get out of here? I am really tired,” I said, making a face.

“Okay, foxy, which one did you like then? Like other than the bodycon dress because I am buying it for your upcoming dates.” Myra said, smiling.

“You won’t stop, right? Why do I bother? I like the polka dot one. It’s comfy and a dress so why the hell not?” I said feeling confident about myself.

“Yeah also the polka dot one is the definition of fancy but not too fancy,” Myra said sarcastically.

So we finally decided to buy those dresses and get out of that damm store. As soon as we entered the house Myra screamed, MA WE FOUND THE PERFECT DRESS that almost killed me. I screamed SHUT UP, I yelled because I was half asleep the whole time since we started driving home. Aunty knew it was coming. When I yelled both of them started laughing and that kinda pissed me off but I was way too tired to deal with both of them.

“Arohi my dear you must be exhausted, have some water and take a little nap. I will wake you up when dinner is ready.” said aunt with concern. “Myra today you are gonna help me come on.” aunt ordered.

"Ugh, mom, okay fine. Anyways, tomorrow is Arohi's day so I will help you. Aarohi you take some rest." Myra said, giving me a smirk.

I was too tired to think of replying to Myra's comment and decided to just let it go, so I just thanked my aunt and warned Myra to keep her voice in control.

After a while

"WAKE UP. THE DINNER IS READY." Myra screamed at the top of her lungs.

THREE

Not a Date

"AAROHI WAKE UP, WAKE UP. IT'S ALMOST 11." Myra screamed at the top of her lungs.

"WHAT THE HECK MYRA" I screamed back at her, and she shocked me from inside. "Stop screaming please, for god's sake." I pleaded. "Wait, what did you just say? is it 11? Seriously? You are an idiot! it's 10 Myra, how is it almost 11?" I screamed again.

"You have a date to get ready for Aarohi," Myra said in excitement.

"How many times do I have to tell you, it's not a date," I said getting out of bed.

"Okay okay fine not a date, but you still have to get ready. I thought you wanted to look like a girl so don't you think you will need at least an hour for that?" Myra said, staring at me."Plus, when are you leaving? is he coming to pick you up?" Myra asked, raising her eyebrows at me.

"Oh, Myra, I bought that dress. That's enough girly stuff. I am gonna go take a bath and get dressed and that's it. And yes he is coming here to pick me up." I said, rubbing my eyes and forcing myself to walk towards the bathroom.

"He is picking you up and you say it's not a date," Myra said, with a smirk on her face.

"Bye Myra. I am not even sure why we were having this conversation." I said closing the door of the bathroom.

I don't remember when I slept yesterday. Yesterday night was just different. I don't know how to explain what I felt but I think I finally found someone who understands me other than Myra and aunt. We kept on talking about random things and never ran out of topics to talk about.

I got ready and texted Vihaan to check if he was ready and to ask him when he was gonna leave. Surprisingly he texted me back within a minute and asked me to meet him outside my house. I rushed towards the door but Myra being Myra opened the door before I could.

"Oh my god" screamed Myra looking at Vihaan.

"Vihaan this is the screamy sleepyhead I was talking about," I said smiling.

"Hey there," Vihaan said shyly, smiling at Myra.

"Umm hey," Myra said, not taking her eyes off Vihaan.

"Aarohi let's get going, shall we?" Said Vihaan looking at me.

This brought Myra back to reality. She was a little offbeat when Vihaan said that and I could sense that.

"Yes right, you guys should get going," Myra said hesitating.

Vihaan and I headed to the cafe nearby.

"Hey, you're different today. I mean you look great today. So went with the girly look huh? That necklace don't you have it since forever?" said Vihaan looking straight at my eyes.

"You are quite the observer huh? Thanks though. You don't look so bad yourself, blue is your colour. Also, this necklace was my mum's. She loved these Quartz Crystals and all, so she had many of them. I wore this one because it was her favourite. It makes me feel like she is around me." I said with a lot of emotions rushing through me.

"Aarohi you okay? Are you sure you are gonna be okay with sharing things like these? I know these wounds are too fresh even if they happened years ago, it feels like someone cut you yesterday. It's okay if you wanna take the time okay and know that I am ready to listen to whatever you have to say whenever you want to say okay?" Vihaan said, holding my hands within his, with so much concern in his voice.

"I seriously cannot thank you enough Vihaan, you have no idea what you just did. This means a lot, thank you." I said with tears in my eyes. "Vihaan don't you think we should tell Myra the truth now?" I said suddenly before he could say anything.

"I know we should but Myra would have overreacted and you said she believed the friend's story also your aunt already knows, doesn't she?" Vihaan said.

"Yes but I hate it. I never hide anything from her. I want her to know everything, please can we tell her? Also, we can't hide this forever, right? And what exactly are you afraid of?" I said, smiling at him.

"Yeah you are right but she has no idea who I am right? You know exactly what I am afraid of, don't try acting all innocent." Vihaan said, making a face.

"She never asked. it's actually very unlike her but maybe she forgot your name, after all, we only met once or twice when we were like 10. I mean when I was 10. She was just 8. Come on, what do you expect? You were\are the oldest so you remember." I said.

"Yeah, not too old though I was just 13. I am kinda tensed. I hope she will be okay with going into the past, also is it gonna be okay with you to describe the whole story to us all?" Vihaan asked with concern in his eyes.

"I hope so. I will be okay and if not then you, aunt and Myra are there to help me, you know what to do right?" I said, taking a deep breath.

"Yeah, I do know what to do. I just hope we don't have to do that. Umm, can I ask you something Aarohi?" Vihaan sighed.

"Yeah sure, what is it?"

"Why do you all of a sudden wanna talk about this?" Vihaan said, looking blankly at my face.

"Because my therapist has been trying hard but I don't think I can open up to her and I have been thinking of opening up to someone and who else is better than you all!? Plus I recently read this somewhere "if you don't heal you will bleed on the people who didn't cut you" and I guess I do wanna heal now. Ahh enough with this, that waiter is staring at us for a long time, let's order something before they kick us out, so what do you wanna eat?" I asked him as I stared at the Menu.

"Umm doughnuts, you? By the way, you are still really good at changing subjects huh? I like that." Vihaan said keeping the menu down.

"I would love me some donuts. I hope everything will be okay, I am a little scared Vihaan. Okay, a lie, I am very scared." I said

"it will be okay Aarohi. I will be by your side, I won't leave your side ever again now. I promise and you know I am not lying, right? Also if want we can take this all slow let's talk about all this later, there is no rush right?" said Vihaan with a soft voice and concern in his eyes

"Yeah I know you are here and I am thankful for that but this is just scary, opening up about my feelings isn't my thing you know that. I just don't want to feel all the same things I felt earlier. it was really hard for me to get away from it and to completely let go of everything. To accept that it happened. I have been feeling very good after that and I feel like if I share, it will make me feel better. Also, Miss Sima always wants me to share. I never really could open up to her, not about my past. We just talk about what I feel now because of it and how I could let it go. She helped me a lot but I just cannot make myself open up to her." I said with a small smile on my face.

"That's okay, hey hey Aarohi, don't rush yourself it's okay to have your walls built up, I understand what this all is coming from. I have been there myself so I know exactly what is happening with you. You can take some more time. Don't feel guilty about not letting others know who you are because that was just a part of your past, it wasn't a part of you, right? it's okay to take time to open up about things. Those are the scars you have owned for years and I know how deep scars could be, we all know that and we are here for you okay?" Vihaan said, smiling back at me.

"You just made me more confident about talking about this now. it's time now. I want to share my scars. I want you all to know my side of the story, I never talked to her or anybody about this personally and now I want to, I don't want to wait anymore, I want you aunt and Myra to hear me out." I said with a bright face.

"That's fair enough but make sure you can take it okay? I don't want you to go through those things again just know it's okay if you need more time, stop whenever you feel like it's too much," said Vihaan with a shaky voice.

"It's you guys, my family. I want you to know me. I do, I will be okay." I said with confidence on my face.

"As long as you are okay with it, so am I," Vihaan said with a smile on his face.

"Thanks for being there even when I was not the easiest to handle, thanks for dealing with my craziness, thanks for never leaving my side, even when you were so far you were the closest to me. I hope you know I love you Vihaan. I don't know how I got so lucky to have you in my life. I am just glad I have you in my life." I said with tears in my eyes.

"Hey don't cry you, idiot, it's okay. Chill, that's what family is supposed to do: love you, be there for you, support you no matter what and that's exactly what I did. I acted according to my role and just like you are I am lucky to have you and aunt by my side too, so don't cry now." Vihaan said as he wiped my tears away.

"Let's finish these delicious donuts and get the hell out of here," I said changing the subject.

" Yes, sure. By the way, you are still very good at it aren't you?." Vihaan said, smiling at me. "Wanna go walk around like lost puppies?" Vihaan asked with so much excitement in his eyes.

"Um, I don't know Vihaan," I said feeling bad about not accepting his offer.

"Oh come on Aarohi." Vihaan insisted.

"Okay fine. Let's go, you are not gonna listen to me anyway, are you?" I said making a face.

"Nup never not about this. Come on, you know how much I love walking and I have been waiting to do that with you forever." Vihaan said, staring at me like a puppy.

"That's right, let's just go. Come on, we gotta take Myra and aunt donuts too!" I said as I got out of my seat.

"Yeah," Vihaan said as he got up.

After wandering around like some lost puppies, for a while we decided to head home.

"I am gonna talk about things now once we reach home I hope you are free?" I said breaking the silence.

"Yes, of course, I am always free for you Aarohi," said Vihaan in a calm voice.

The rest of the ride home was kind of silent.

FOUR

THE STRANGE DAY

"ANUT, MYRA" I screamed. I am home and I wanna talk with you guys and Vihaan." I said in a low voice.

"OMG! Aarohi chill you scared the crap out of me, what is it? You and Vihaan are getting married or what?" Myra said, looking straight into my eyes.

"Shut up Myra and listen to me," I said with a bossy accent.

"Oh, you girls are such a headache sometimes. What do you want to talk about Aarohi?" asked my aunt.

"I wanna talk about my story. I wanna tell you guys my story by myself. I think I am ready for it now." I said as I looked at them.

"Aarohi are you sure? Like are you sure about telling us your story?" my aunt asked with concern in her eyes.

"MA this is what you ask her? She just called Vihaan one of us, you just met him Aarohi. How did that happen?"

"That's exactly why I want you to know my story. Each one of you only knows a part of it. That too by your side so I want you all to know my story from my side." I said as I took a deep breath.

"If you are sure then go for it Aarohi," Vihaan said.

"Thanks, Vihaan," I said giving Vihaan a sign.

FIVE

UNREAL

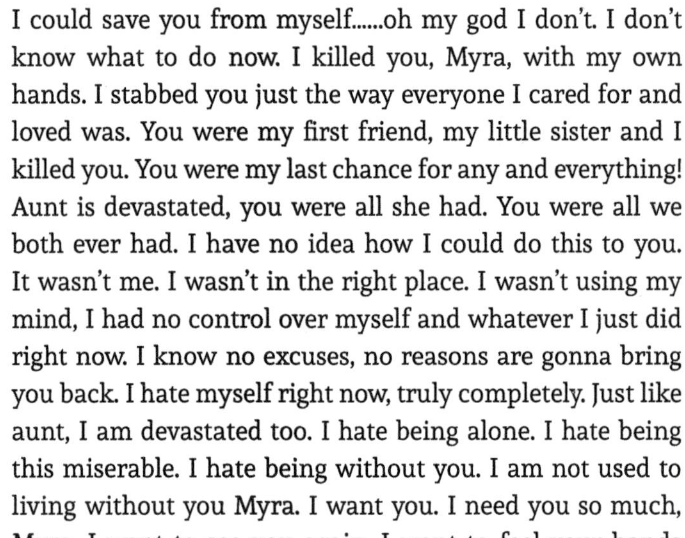

Why did I do this? How did I do this? I.....I killed you. I wish I could save you from myself......oh my god I don't. I don't know what to do now. I killed you, Myra, with my own hands. I stabbed you just the way everyone I cared for and loved was. You were my first friend, my little sister and I killed you. You were my last chance for any and everything! Aunt is devastated, you were all she had. You were all we both ever had. I have no idea how I could do this to you. It wasn't me. I wasn't in the right place. I wasn't using my mind, I had no control over myself and whatever I just did right now. I know no excuses, no reasons are gonna bring you back. I hate myself right now, truly completely. Just like aunt, I am devastated too. I hate being alone. I hate being this miserable. I hate being without you. I am not used to living without you Myra. I want you. I need you so much, Myra. I want to see you again. I want to feel your hands on mine again, I need to hear your laugh, I need to see your bright smile and that cute dimple. I need to hear you scream. I need you, Myra. I need to hear you say that " It's gonna be okay, that I am gonna be okay" Myra oh Myra! I cannot believe this. How on earth can I kill you? I never thought in my worst nightmare that I would do something like this. I always saw myself killing myself but you? Never Myra I mean this Never. God, you are so far away from me. And the thought that I can never see you again is killing me all over again. I can do nothing to change it anymore. I can do nothing to bring you back Myra. I feel so helpless. I don't know what to think or do anymore. The worst part is all I remember is stabbing you. I fainted immediately after that. And all I came to know when I woke up was that you were gone....forever. Because of me. Because I killed you! ***I fucking killed you, Myra.*** How can I do this? How can I kill you? I don't even think I am alive anymore.

Aunt hated me and she said "You are bad luck Aarohi. You are the reason everything has happened. First, you let your dog die, you could have done something to save him right? Then your father died, followed by your mother. That bloody Purab died too just because he let you live. I am sure that's the only reason God killed him. I wish he killed you instead of them. Then I wouldn't have to take care of you, you were nothing but a burden to me. I was going through such a rough time yet I had to be there for you. I had to stop my therapy to be able to pay for yours. And now you showed us that it was nothing but a waste of my money and you killed my daughter, your sister who accepted her fate and let you in. You killed her. How could you?"

Vihaan loved Myra. He liked her with all his heart. I know this because all he kept talking about on the way back home was her. He thought I wasn't listening but I was. I heard everything. He was angry and devastated. He never screamed at me but today was an exception for everything. He screamed at me and blamed me for everything, his father dying, destroying aunt's life and for killing Myra.

He isn't wrong, no one is wrong other than me. They both are speaking facts for the first time but it hurts more because I never thought they could be so harsh to me. I am too used to their love and care. It's all my fault and I know and own it but it isn't gonna be enough. They both are gonna hate me forever and I can do nothing about it. I have no one anymore. No one will stand by me, understand me, love me, and care for me. I am gonna be all alone and lonely all over again.

All Myra asked me to do was to take my meds but I kept denying them even when I knew I had to take them. I felt as if she wanted to make fun of my state. I never believed in medicines to cure mental illness. I always knew I just had to get it out of my system. "Pain demands to be felt" I read this quote somewhere and I just couldn't forget it. I tried opening up but I couldn't. I wanted someone close to me to know about my story. It was really hard to talk about it. I don't know why but it made me feel unsafe. It made me feel as if people close to me would push me away thinking it was all my fault, thinking that I bring bad luck to people, as I felt responsible for everything happening around me. And that's exactly what happened when I talked about all this. I knew it would affect me but I never thought it would affect me so much that I would kill Myra. No one did anything for me. Vihaan used to visit me sometimes but they never really got inside. They blamed me for everything yet they knew that it broke me too.

Now I am just wondering about how my life is gonna be now. Now everything seems to be ending, now that everything seems to be gone, now that everything's so messed up. I don't know how long it has been since I left this place, the window of my bedroom. It has always been my hanging spot for my entire life. I used to come here because it made me who I am, it was my happy place but to my surprise, I haven't been myself lately. Even when all I do is sit here. I have not read a book not even a single quote, I haven't eaten since I don't know when I haven't talked to anyone, I haven't seen anyone for a while now not even my family, I haven't showered nor have I brushed my teeth. I haven't heard anything other than the stillness in the room and sometimes people banging on the door as if they were trying to break inside, but no one ever dared to do so as if they knew what they would see. See me in this broken state, broken is underestimating what I felt. It is more than that. I never thought my heart could be this damaged, I never thought I would be this hurt, this broken that I can no longer feel anything left inside me. In the mornings or the afternoons I could feel my blood vessels burning up my whole body, in the chilly nights or evenings I could feel my body freezing up but despite all this, it couldn't move me, not even by an inch. Sometimes I use to feel the rain droplets on my face as if nature wanted me to cry, wanted me to show it that I wasn't dead. I haven't cried since that day. I just couldn't. I felt the pain but no tears could justify how bad it was. After many hours, days or weeks the pain faded away but left me with emptiness. Maybe it left me because I was too used to it, maybe because I was too comfortable with it, maybe because I started being okay with it. The emptiness was surprisingly more disturbing and weakening than the pain I had felt earlier. At first, I lived with misery but now I am the misery. I never felt this empty. It's not like I haven't felt pain or emptiness, I have! I survived depression, anxiety, loneliness and whatnot. I fought it all and it has made me nothing but stronger. I never thought anything could break me again. I thought I was so broken that nothing could ever break me again but I guess I was wrong, perhaps I was always wrong. I never knew losing someone could affect you this much. I never thought losing her would affect me this much. Everything is a blur since that day I don't know how many days have passed by. I was so shocked by this news I just couldn't handle it. I wish things could have been different for us. I wish I could have been a little more careful about things, a little more of myself. I wish I wouldn't have been so foolish, I wish I could have saved you from my thoughts, from myself. I wish I could go back in time and trust you a little more, maybe you would still be by my side. I should have trusted you a little more, maybe I wouldn't have lost you today. Maybe you could have fixed me someday. You were my last hope, my last wish and maybe my last love and I lost you. ***I lost you. Maybe I was never meant to be fixed!***

SIX

CONFUSION

Is she going to be an okay doctor? She hasn't moved for a few hours.

She will be okay. But you all have to take extra good care of her once she wakes up. I suggest you all meet her one by one.

Yes doctor we will take good care of her.

She is awake. One of you can meet her.

Maa, you should go in first.

Yes aunt you should go in first.

Aunt enters Aarohi's room

"Aunt" I screamed.

"You are here to see me? Wait where am I? Is this a hospital?" I asked with confusion.

"Of course, I came to see you Aarohi. Yes, this is a hospital you fainted yesterday night so we brought you here and ever since then we all are here with you."

"I what? How did you know I fainted? And who else is here with you aunt?"

"Aarohi you fainted so we got you to the hospital immediately. Vihaan and-"

"Of course, he called you and he must have brought me here after."

"Yes, dear, he did. But he didn't call me. I was there with him when you fainted. We all were there."

"Aunt, how were you there with me?"

"Dear, don't you remember? You were going to tell us about your past and-"

"I know aunt and I feel terrible about it." I said as i started crying.

"Aarohi my dear child, I know how you feel I get it. It wasn't your fault, don't feel otherwise you just tried to push your limits and maybe pushed too far."

My aunt suddenly was behaving as if nothing happened. She was acting like before. I don't know how she could do that. How can someone forgive such a bastard like me? Someone who killed her daughter. Maybe she forgave me because I am the only thing she is left with. Only one who she can call family. Maybe because she loved me too hard to lose me too. Maybe because she sees me as her daughter again. Only a mother can forgive someone for such a deed but how can she love me so much?

I feel so guilty. I don't want to live anymore. I don't think I deserve to live anymore. It's almost as if I lost the only switch to my humanity forever. Without it. Without her. I am gonna be a total mess. A total loser. An emotionless body. A living yet dead person.

"Aarohi I am gonna send Vihaan in now is that okay with you?"

"Umm yes, aunty it's okay with me."

Oh god, who knows how he is gonna react? I hope he is okay. Who am I kidding? He is gonna be devastated. I know he liked her. He liked Myra and I killed her. I killed her in front of him. His sister whom he adored and loved killed someone in front of him.

"Hey, aarohi! I am so happy to see you awake and well alive. Don't take this the wrong way. Seriously, I am really happy to see you. Are you feeling okay now? " Vihaan said nervously

"I am feeling okay now. You are happy to see me? Are you sure about that? " I said getting all teared up

"Of course, I am, why wouldn't I be happy? After all, you are my sister! " said Vihaan smiling a little

How can he be so selfless, so loving and so caring? This is too much love and affection that I am receiving. I don't deserve this, I do not! How can they both act as if I died? Maybe it's because they think I tried to commit suicide. Did I? Why can't I remember what exactly was the last memory I have in my mind before waking up here? It's all such a blur.

"Aarohi I am gonna send Myra in okay?" said Vihaan normally

"WHAT!?"

SEVEN

WHAT!?

What is he thinking? I mean I get that he is angry and all but seriously why is he fucking around with such a sensitive subject!? I know he cared about her and that he liked her but this is taking it too far! I miss her too I care about her too, doesn't he realise that? Being sarcastic about something like this is so horrible god hates this

"What are you talking about Vihaan!? Myra? Did you just say, Myra? Seriously you think it's a thing to fuck around with? " I gasped

What am I even thinking I hate myself for what I did. I killed her I deserve every cruelty, every wrong and bad thing in this world nothing is too much for what I did anymore!

"Aarohi I know you thought she was making fun of you but she wasn't, trust me she means no harm to you. She is your sister after all. Come on, meet her once, you will feel better too." Vihaan said making a puppy face.

"What are you talking about Vihaan? Myra? Do you want me to meet Myra? How is that even possible? How on earth can I ever meet Myra again!?" I almost screamed this time.

"Why not Aarohi? I know you might still be mad at her but..." I cut vihaan halfway through.

"Mad at her? What are you talking about Vihaan? If I could, I would hug her and apologise for everything I did to her." I said almost crying.

"Well, Aarohi guess what? You have a chance to talk to her and so you can meet her and apologise too but only if you want, okay? " Vihaan said getting up.

"What are you talking about!?" I asked confused.

"Wait here, let me send Myra in," he said almost rushing out.

"Wait what sent Myra in are you kidding me? Vihaan wait!!" I screamed.

Myra? What is he talking about? How can I or even he meet Myra again? Is he hallucinating things? I am really worried about him now.

"Sorry, um Vihaan. Why don't you send aunt in for a bit? Please, I need to talk to her first." I said as calmly as I could.

"Sure Aarohi, why not?" he managed to say with a smile.

"Aunt! Is Vihaan okay? Is he hallucinating things? Should we let a doctor see him?" I said almost as soon as she entered the room.

As soon as I said that I realised how I needed one, it made me feel fragile.

"What are you talking about, Aarohi?" aunt asked nervously.

"He wants me to meet Myra I don't get-" anut cut me halfway through

"Aarohi I get it, that you got mad at her and don't want to talk to her but you really should otherwise you will feel bad and she will too." said anut patting my shoulder.

What? I don't understand any of this. Why are they both acting like this? Is aunt hallucinating too?

"Aunt" I called her out helplessly.

"Yes, Beta?" she said with concern in her voice.

"Can I see the doctor?" I said with a straight face.

"Sure beta. It's almost time for your check-up too," she said as she got going.

"Dr Sima, everyone from my family wants me to meet Myra. I don't understand how I or anyone else can do that?" I said with irritation.

"Why Aarohi? Did she do anything to you? Did you guys fight? Is she the reason you had to come here?" she asked, looking into my eyes.

"No. That's not it. Doc but how am I supposed to meet her now? I was always scared of hurting people, hurting myself but I never thought I would do such a thing. "I said holding back tears.

"What are you talking about? We still need to run some tests just to be sure but I think you are hallucinating it can be PTSD."

"What are you talking about I ain't the one who is hallucinating it is them doc they want me to meet Myra, I CAN'T MEET MYRA!" I screamed.

"Why can't you meet Myra Aarohi?"

"Cause I stabbed her just the way they were stabbed." I cried

"What are you talking about Aarohi?" she said purposefully

"She is no more! I killed her. I killed her." I screamed and cried.

"Aarohi my dear, you haven't killed anyone okay? Relax I don't know what exactly was your hallucination and what you went through but I am sure that the reality is better than that. So drink some water and be grateful that whatever you think you did isn't real" she said calmly.

"What are you trying to say?" I was confused sad and happy at the same time.

"Myra-"

" Myra is ALIVE? Myra is alive?" I said with a lot of hope and doubt.

"Yes, Aarohi she is alive. You were hallucinating when you thought you killed Myra. but the reality is that Myra is totally fine. She is here waiting to meet you. I know this is a lot for you but it's good news that she is alive, isn't it? So take deep breaths as I told you to do and once you feel better, I will send her in." doc said.

"Okay." was all I managed to say.

That's all I managed to say even though I wanted to scream at my doc I wanted to scream at the world but I just said okay. What was happening to me, to my brain, why on earth would my brain want to make me think I killed Myra? And what is this doc saying, already talking to her was the worst of all yet somehow I got used to doing it, even though I didn't do much talking I did accept her and her methods even though I hate it. Needing to eat pills is the worst of it all. Now she will give me more of them and now I have to meet her more than once a week. I hate this, I hate her! What if my brain is now comforting me by making me hallucinate, I mean dream this all? Or whatever doc is saying is true? I would like to believe the second reality, it sounds a lot better. If she is telling me the truth and it's not just one of those therapy shit, then I would want to see Myra again. That will prove everything, won't it?

"Please can you send her in right now" I hurried as I got back into the reality

The doc left the room and I was with my thoughts again. So Myra isn't dead. I didn't kill her. Umm okay Wow. How is that even possible? It all felt so real. I am glad she is alive. She is here. I can meet her! I don't know how to react! What should I do? Apposilzse for killing her which I never actually did? Hug her? I don't know. To be honest this doesn't feel real that she is alive. I can believe it all when I see her.

"Aarohi?" said Myra with hesitation.

That's Myra's voice! Hearing her voice never made me feel so happy ever. My heart is melting. I want to see her but I am afraid I will do something to her. She is my little sister. My best friend. I cannot let her down again. She is here to meet her sister and her best friend and I am gonna give her that. I cannot keep making this about me every time. This time it's about her. I just hope this is the actual reality. I hope I can see her.

"Myra! I missed you so much. I know it's not been much time for you but me, it's been days, weeks and months apart from you, aunt and Vihaan. I thought that I would never meet you again, at least not in this life. I am really glad I could see you again, I can feel your arms around me again, I could see that sparkle in your eyes again, I can see your bright smile again. I need to know exactly how much you mean to me and I still have you in my life. People only realise someone's value when they lose them and Myra I lost you forever and now that I see you again every memory we made together, everything we shared and everything that has happened with us just makes me feel more grateful than ever before" I said Is I cried.

"Oh, Aarohi you have no idea how we all are feeling since the second you fainted we all thought it was because we did something. Especially me, Aarohi. I was supposed to help you get out of this more than anyone else. And I felt like I am the one who dragged you in this more. You didn't even want to meet me and it broke me so bad. But

I didn't know what you were going through. You are even more broken Aarohi. I could never imagine a world without you. I don't know how you got through those days but now I am here with you and I am not leaving your side okay? " said Myra as she cried.

"You have no idea how much comfort this just gave me. I feel complete again. I feel like a huge weight got off my chest. The fact that you no longer exist because of me, just killed me every second."

"Hey, Aarohi? You can never kill me okay? Don't think so much about it now. You have me here with you, right? Then what are you worried about now? We will get through this together." said Myra wiping her tears.

"Myra, I am just happy that it was whatever it was and not reality that's it. That's all I wanted or could have asked for." I said smiling at her.

"I am just glad you are okay." she said while she hugged me.

"Did Dr Sima tell you all that exactly happened?" I asked nervously.

"No, she said she will tell us all together about it," Myra said simply.

"Okay, where is she now? She is outside talking with Ma and Vihaan. I will let them know that they can come in. I hope that's okay with you." Myra said with hope in her eyes.

"Yes yes, it is please call them in," I said eagerly.

"Hello Aarohi, how are you feeling now?" Asked doc

"I am feeling good. Doc you were wrong, I felt better once I saw her, I didn't have to feel better before," I said smiling at her.

"What happened was Aarohi thought she killed Myra. Yes, she hallucinated killing her. I don't know the details as I haven't talked to her about it but we will cover it all in the upcoming therapy session. But for now, you all need to know that this isn't as easy as we thought." she said as tho I wasn't even in the room.

Myra started crying

Aunt and Vihaan tried to calm her down. But she kept crying.

"Aarohi you wanna say something?" said doc looking at me.

I nodded a no

That's good. I want to tell you all about PTSD, as I think that is the case here. Post-traumatic stress disorder (PTSD) is a disorder that develops in some people who have experienced a shocking, scary, or dangerous event. It is natural to feel afraid during and after a traumatic situation. Fear triggers many split-second changes in the body to help defend against danger or to avoid it. People with PTSD have intense, disturbing thoughts and feelings related to their experience that last long after the traumatic event has ended. They may relive the event through flashbacks or nightmares.

"Okay," I said with no emotions.

"Yes, for now, Aarohi please take a rest, you're gonna have a long day tomorrow. Tomorrow we can start your treatment based on this" she said and left the room.

I don't know what I am supposed to do or think now. I had such a hard time opening up to Dr Sima. I rarely talked about anything, just took the pills she gave me. I don't know how having to talk even more to her is gonna work for me. I don't know how she will react to the feelings I have inside me, the feelings which are buried so deep that even I get lost inside them sometimes, even I forget the way out of them at times. Will she ever really understand what I feel and why I feel that way? Will she be able to help me? Will this disease ever leave my side? I don't wanna feel the pain I felt when I thought I killed Myra! Wait! What if this is just my mind making this all up so I feel less pain, so I get out of the guilt I was drowning in? The guilt was about to explode in my body and take me down with it. What if this isn't the actual reality and the reality is that I killed Myra? My thoughts know no bounds. I am going crazy but I am in real confusion. What can I do to change anything though? There is nothing I can do to know what the actual reality is. I guess I should just try to sleep. Maybe I will wake beside the window this time as I did in the hospital the first time.

EIGHT

FINALLY

Seems like whatever I saw yesterday is the truth. So that just means that I have to take the therapy as something is wrong with my brain, I am seeing things that don't happen and I am pretty much capable of seeing anything, all I know is that I can't trust what I see. I can never figure out the truth. I might live the false life happily while everyone I care about suffers or I suffer while everyone else is happy and the only reason for their unhappiness is me. I don't want both. I want to be happy with my loved ones, I want to cry with them, I want to laugh with them, I want to live with them. I want to see what they see. Yet there is nothing I can do to fix this, to fix me.

"Good Morning Aarohi," said doc

"Umm yes morning doc" I said even though I don't see why it's good.

"Aarohi my dear, Be ready to change your life around, to change the way you see life, the way you live life. We will start our session in 5 okay? I will be back, I need to talk to Dr Vaze a little." said doc

That sure sounds good but I don't know if that can happen. We will see.

"Okay," I said with no emotions.

"It's okay, I am here only to help you Aarohi. Okay?"

"Yes, I get that."

That's the only thing getting me. Why do I need help? Why can't I work like a normal human being? What's so wrong with me that I need help? Why can't I help myself? Why is it so hard for me to just be normal? Why do I need someone to tell me and explain to me who I am, why can't I know it by myself? It hurts so bad. Why can't I stop feeling like a burden, failure, weak, helpless and so fragile? I hate feeling like this. I am supposed to talk to her. Okay, that's just great! Back to talking to a so-called known stranger about how they were killed, how I am a very very stupid person who is now mentally ill, sounds fun!

This wasn't the first time I was going to talk to a therapist but it felt worst, my anxiety knew no bounds and my head kept telling me to run away as I saw the doc entering the room. I don't want this I don't want to talk to her about how I feel or about my life anymore. I couldn't even talk about it to my family the closest people to me why does everyone think I can talk to her? I don't want to go through all the therapy sessions again. It took a while to go to one session per week now it will have to increase again and now the dosage of the meditation is gonna be Heavy too. I don't like taking pills and talking to a shrink like I am a crazy person. I hate this so much, I hate her so much. I hate myself too, why on earth am I seeing things that don't exist!?

"Hello, Aarohi," said doc smiling at me.

It felt sarcastic as if she was smiling at my situation and how being in therapy hasn't helped me even a bit.

"Hi," I said controlling every emotion in me

"Can we talk about what exactly happened that day?"

God, why does she think pushing my buttons is the solution always? I don't like this I don't fucking remember what happened only if knew I would be sane and I wouldn't need her. Dear lord why does she have to push me like this?

"Umm I am not sure about what happened" I replied with no emotions

"Don't you remember anything before you fainted?"

"No" I lied.

I didn't feel like talking to her. I remember everything, a little too clearly for that matter.

"I think I am going to talk to your aunt and talk to you after," the doc said

"Okay," I said and looked away

This is ridiculous just when I thought this cannot get any worst it just did. She is now gonna talk to every one of them. That's just great I wasn't troubled enough now they have to go through therapy cause of me. Just great! I wished to stop her but I knew she wouldn't listen so I just let it be.

NINE

PANIC

She came in the next day and said "I have talked to them and they told me everything that happened so would you like to say something?"

What does she want? Didn't she just say she knows what happened? Why does she want me to relive my trauma? What is wrong with her, God? I don't wanna talk, but I guess I have to. "I fainted when I tried to talk about my past," I said not looking at her. Cause I knew I was a disappointment. At least for myself, I was, I hate myself for that. For everything. For not being able to let anyone in. For being nothing but trouble and pain for others. I hate myself. I hate that they all have to go through such things because of me, even so, I still don't get better but I just got worse.

"Okay, why do you think that happened? Why do you think it's so hard for you to express that part of yourself?" She asked simply

What now? Of course, Cause it's heartbreaking I hate to think of them. It makes my heart beat faster and I relive all the trauma again I am trying not to think of it right now but I cannot help it. Gosh, imma have a panic attack.

I said nothing but I still got a panic attack. What did she do? Gave me a pill to swallow and some water. I hate her too. I hate her so much, I hate those pills. I feel like a crazy person. I am not crazy, am I? I don't want to be a crazy person, I cannot stop panicking why is this happening to me? God someone please stop this.

"Hey hey calm down beta, here hold my hand and squeeze it, if it is too much okay? Trying to breathe and drink water slowly." Said Dr Vaze as he handed me a glass of water.

"Thank you" I said plainly as I gulped some water

"Drink it slowly beta so it calms you down as it goes in," he said with concern.

I tried again and it helped me calm down a little. No one has ever helped my nerves calm down like this before. How, how did he do that? Is this so easy to overcome stuff like that? How did I just stop my panic halfway through?

"Did you take your pill?" Dr Vaze said breaking the strom of thoughts in my mind

"No," I said as I sighed

Yet another doctor with pills, god when will this nightmare end?

"Don't you think the pills calm you down?" Said Dr Vaze as if he knew why I sighed.

I was surprised at the question he had just asked me.

"It does help me calm down but it doesn't feel natural," I said immediately

He smiled.

I was embarrassed and I wanted to dig a hole and hide inside it. But I couldn't and I didn't know what to do. I felt kinda stupid but saying that out loud felt kinda nice.

"I see yet another rebel for pills. It's okay to feel that way but remember these are for you, to make you feel better, to make it easier for you. Not to make uncomfortable or uneasy. They just make the process faster but of course, if you work with them, they are useless on their own. So don't wait for the pills to do the work, try doing it yourself. " He said as he stroked my head and smiled looking at me.

Whatever he just said made too much sense. He made me feel comfortable and open, he was being real and honest yet everything felt like a dream. His words comforted me and gave me a sense of reality yet I didn't wish to run away. It calmed me down instantly as I realised I was in charge, I was in control it made me feel so much better. I didn't feel helpless after such a long time. I looked at him and smiled for the first time in a while. There was a warmth in his smile, which made me feel joy, I didn't know what joy was at the time but I felt it very deeply. For the first time in a while, I felt human.

Then I was forced to gulp some more pills later in the day and at night. As I expected the dosage was now increased. It made me feel sleepy and I didn't like that. Felt like I was doing drugs even when I didn't want to. Yet I was still looking forward to tomorrow maybe just maybe I will get a chance to meet Dr Vaze again. He has been so kind to me but I didn't even get a chance to thank him properly.

TEN

DR VAZE

As soon as I woke up, I got dressed and ready. I took my meds even before the nurse came by. I was waiting for the doc to come or maybe perhaps Dr Vaze to pass by. I don't know why I was so excited I just was and to be honest I liked it for a change. I was thinking about something else other than the things my head was showing me and how I was a disaster so that was a relief.

I saw doc passing by and I was so happy to see her. I called her out and she was as shocked as I was. She still came in.

"What's wrong Aarohi?" she raised her eyebrows.

"Where is Dr Vaze?" I asked ignoring her question completely.

She looked at me puzzled and then said "He will soon be on his rounds"

I was happy to hear that and gave her a big smile "Thanks"

She looked at me and then asked me if I had taken my meds, I said I had so she left. Just after a while, I saw her talking to Dr Vaze.

I was early waiting for him to show up and to my surprise he did! He came in!

"Hellooo" I almost screamed with excitement.

"Hello beta," He said as he gave me his calming smile.

"I wanted to thank you for before" I said hesitating

"Oh that, don't mention it. I didn't do anything it was all you"

"No, but without you, I wouldn't have been able to do it"

"It's nothing like that beta, see I was here to make you understand what was happening. When you understood that you did the rest yourself. You don't need me for this but me being here just makes it easier. Okay?"

I was shocked. He just said the most simple words but they felt very Heavy. I was silent for a while but then I smiled at him. He smiled back.

"I am gonna go meet my other clients now okay? I will see you around kid." He said and left.

That's when it clicked to me. HIS CLIENTS! I could be one of them. I wanna be under his wing. I am sure it will be very good for me. Now I just have to convince him and doc.

I was gonna meet Mrya in the evening. I was ready to talk about this, changing therapist.

"MYRA" I screamed when I saw her

She shushed me and came in rushing.

"This better be good Aarohi," she said giving me a look.

" IT IS. I talked to Dr Vaze again and it was so good. He just says words with such simplicity yet they seem to be of greatest knowledge."

"It's good to see you so excited about a therapist"

This was the first time I thought of Dr Vaze as a therapist. Till now I just saw him as a father figure and not as a Doctor even tho I call him Dr Vaze he seemed like someone close to me.

"Therapist yeah," I said smiling.

"Aarohi are you sure you want this change, if so I will talk to both of them today"

"I am very sure Myra"

"Great then I will go talk to the doc and Dr Vaze"

“Okay,” I said excitedly

Myra left and all I could think was about how they both will react to this. I was excited yet very nervous.

“Hey doc, can I talk to you for a while?” Myra asked

“Yes sure Myra what is it?” the doc said smiling

“Aarohi seems changed since she meet Dr Vaze, she is willing to talk about things she is just more-”

“alive?” interrupted doc

“YES,” said Myra

“Yes, I get where this is going and I have already talked with Dr Vaze. He said he was okay with it.” the doc said

“But are you okay with this?” Myra asked hesitantly

“Ofc Myra. it is my job to make sure Aarohi gets better, I want what’s best for her. It is okay if I am not it, this isn’t something I should take personally. I am happy she feels good talking to someone as even I have seen her struggle with that a lot. I hope she gets better soon.” she said smiling.

“Thank you doc, you have done a lot for all of us. Really thank you so much. What can I do to make this change possible” Said Myra

“Don’t worry about it, me and Dr Vaze will take care of it, just fill this form and sign it.” the doc said handling the form to Myra

“Okay, thank you again” Myra smiled and left

Myra came in a rush and told me all that happened.

“I am so happy Myra, thank you so much”, I said as I smiled and hugged her

"Come on Aarohi. If not me then who." Myra said as she hugged me back.

Myra and I talked, and after a while, she left. I took my meds on time and I was on my best behaviour. Later in the evening, I was rewarded for my good behaviour.

Dr Vaze came in and I was very delighted to see him.

"HELLO," I said with excitement.

He looked at me and smiled.

"Hello Beta, I see you are feeling good today"

"Yes, yes I am"

"As per your request from now on I will be conducting your therapy sessions okay?" he asked gently.

"Yes, I am looking forward to it," I said with enthusiasm

"I will visit your room mostly at this time, I hope you are taking your meds and eating properly.", he asked with concern

I was a little confused about his question but it felt good. No one has asked me if I had my meal. Everyone only asked me about the meds and if this therapy was working.

"Yes, I had my meal and took my meds" I said with a smile

"Thats good to know Aarohi. Did you have any more panic attacks after we talked that day?" he asked

"No," I said. Noticing it the first time myself.

"That's even better. I see, try listening to what I say carefully, it will help you. Aarohi tell me, what do you like to do?"

He always asked very different questions.

"I like to read, especially poetry" I said with excitement.

"That's great which book have you been reading recently?" he asked simply

That's when it hit me I haven't touched a book in a long time. I was just thinking and thinking so much that I forgot to focus on what I loved the most.

"None," I said with a hint of sadness

"That's okay my child, I just recently read a book I will lend that to you. Give it a try and let me know how it is okay?"

He is always so gentle and sweet. He keeps asking me if things are okay, giving me a chance to tell him my opinion.

"Thank you," I said with a smile on my face again.

"What else do you do to pass your time, something to express yourself?"

I knew something was missing I never realised what, until now. I use to draw as a child, but since the incident tho I had stopped drawing. I kept thinking of it and I kept imagining it, whenever I thought of drawing. But now I had a good image in my mind. I had Myra, Aunt, Vihaan and now even Dr Vaze. I had so much to be grateful for.

"Drawing" I said as tears flow down my eyes.

This was the first time I was being so vulnerable in front of someone. Never did I think I would let myself be this comfortable with just a known stranger. He didn't stop me. He let me cry, he handed me tissues and didn't say a word. His face said "It's gonna be okay, I am here"

"Do you want some water?" he asked me normally

He was acting as if he didn't just see me have a meltdown.

"Yes," I said hesitantly

He handed me the water bottle sitting on the table beside us. I drank a little water and stared at him in question. He didn't say anything. Then I decided to ask him, why he didn't react to my crying.

"Why didn't you react to me crying, make me stop or console me?" I asked in a low voice.

"Because it's an emotion and a way of expressing oneself. It comes naturally to you, even if I ask you to stop, you won't be able to. Plus, there is nothing wrong with crying. It is just being human." he said with a smile.

I had so many things running through my mind, there was a storm of thoughts in my head but with just a few sentences he calmed it down. My head has never listened to anyone not even myself but today, he did it. He looked at me and looked at his watch.

"I will send someone with some art supplies and I will bring a poetry book with me tomorrow okay?"

He asked me before leaving and this made me feel respected and valued.

"Sure, thank you," I said with a smile

"I wanna see a drawing tomorrow, okay?"

I smiled and nodded.

ELEVEN

THE NEW THERAPIEST

"Hi Aarohi," said Doc

"Goodmorning doc," I said smiling at her

"You seem to be in a good mood today"

"Yeah. Can I meet Dr Vaze?" I hurried my way to the question which was bothering me since yesterday night.

"Sadly Aarohi, he isn't going to come for at least the next two days, he is on leave," She said simply.

"Oh okay," I said, as my excitement faded away.

Why isn't he here I really wanna talk to him? I really wanna thank him. Where is he? Why didn't he come?

"Okay so let's start with our session, shall we?" Doc said

I wanted to say no but I couldn't utter a word. I tried, I did but my lips were glued shut. All I could do was nod.

"Aarohi, today we can conduct a test so it helps me understand you better okay?" She said handing me a paper

"Okay," I said and took the paper and saw five questions there. It felt like a joke. You want me to answer five questions and you will understand me better. How? If you cannot even have a conversation with me! Well, whatever I will write that dam test and get this over with.

The first question was "How are you feeling now" there were many words to choose from and I could write only two. And I felt all the opposites, Hopeful and lost. More like Hopeful yet lost. The other questions were mostly about how I think the therapy is working for me and shit. I just wrote what felt like the best choice and gave her the sheet. It felt like it was a review.

"This is it for today. I will see you tomorrow" she said pleased by the answers and left.

I feel like something is missing, for the first time I feel like I am not taking enough effort like I am doing something wrong. I don't know what. I really wanted to meet Dr Vaze. I don't know why but I really do. I guess I just have to wait some more.

The rest of the day was as usual nothing new happened, I took my meds and slept.

The next day was better as it had been a few days since I met anyone other than the staff but today finally I can meet Myra, my aunt and Vihaan. As the doc said that it's okay to meet them. I needed this. I wanna tell Myra everything about Dr Vaze and how he helped me. I wanna reassure aunt and vihaan that I will be fine. I cannot wait to meet them.

“Hey Aarohi” Myra almost screamed with excitement and tears in her eyes and she hugged me

I hugged her back and couldn't control my tears and said "I am so glad to see you all here thank you for coming"

"Are you crazy!? I missed you so much I had to be here." She said as she cried

When my eyes moved from Myra I saw doc staring at us with a notepad and pen in her hand. It creeped me out, that was the moment I knew this wasn't going to be as fun and reliving as I thought it would be. I was being monitored again and all my actions and words were going to be recorded by her. I hated it. I hated her. I didn't want her to walk around with me like a puppy. I tried to ignore her and looked at Vihaan and aunt looking at us. Aunt's eyes filled with tears and Vihaan had an empathetic look on his face.

I talked with aunt and Vihaan and tried to reassure them that I will be fine. I told them that I was doing good and that is the only reason why we were meeting right now. They seem to believe me and gave me a reassuring smile that said that they trusted me.

Vihaan had brought me my necklace and he gave it to me, saying my mother will always be with me no matter what and that just like she trusted me, he trusted me too. Aunt held my hand and told me that she missed my presence and that it was hard handling Myra without me. And we shared a laugh.

I don't know how but when I scanned the room later doc was nowhere to be found and it comforted me. I called Myra and used the opportunity wisely and decided to tell her about Dr Vaze. "Myra" I almost screamed.

Myra immediately came near me and shouted "What happened Aarohi?" with concern in her voice.

"Nothing. I just want to talk to you about something."

Even before Myra could ask me what it was or let me say anything doc came in almost running and ruined everything.

Doc came in and took a scan of the room with a look of disappointment on her face, as tho she wanted me to make a scene. "You all have only a few minutes left," she said and she left.

"What were you gonna say Aarohi?" Myra asked as soon as doc left.

I looked at her and smiled.

"It is getting better here Myra"

"As in? You are talking to doc openly now?" she said excitedly

"No, but I am talking and thinking about things clearly" I said firmly

"Well you aren't being clear right now," said raising her eyebrow.

"Yeah well here is this senior doc. Dr Vaze is an aged man somewhat the same age as my father if he was alive. He has a different aura, he looks young for his age and has a gentle yet bright smile. He legit helped me calm down during a panic attack. He made me feel normal and I like that." I said thinking about it.

"That's so good Aarohi! Can I meet him I really wanna thank him" Myra said

"No that's the things I wanna do but he isn't gonna be here until tomorrow" I said feeling a little sad.

I think Myra sensed that cause she held my hands and gave me a reassuring look and said "It will be alright, you can talk to him tomorrow, don't you worry"

That made me feel happy that I could finally thank him tomorrow. Myra, Aunt and Vihaan left. And the rest of the day was as usual, other than the therapy which wasn't gonna happen today everything was pretty much the same, pills and sleep.

TWELVE

THE DRAWING

“Hello Aarohi,” He said in his calming voice.

“Hello Dr” I said exhausted

“Here is the book I was talking about, Home Body by Rupi Kaur"

“You remembered” I said in shock and smiled at him.

“Of course I do and I also remember something about a drawing,” he said smiling

“Of course, I haven’t forgotten too, I will show it to you,” I said excitedly.

I took the book from the nightstand and showed him the drawing. He kept glancing at it. And after a brief moment, he said “It is amazing, it surely defines who you are doesn’t it?”

“Yes, I think so too” I said thinking of things.

“Why the window?” he asked

"Huh?” I asked in confusion

“Why not a sofa or a bed?” he asked curiously

"Because window connects me with nature and yet never distracts me, rather motivates me to be creative."

"I see. When was the first time you started sitting near a window?"

"Since I started living with Aunt and Myra" I said simply

"Myra and you grew up together?"

"Yeah, pretty much since we were kids"

"I see. And what do you feel about Myra?"

"She is like my sister rather she is my sister. She was there with me through thick and thin. We did have rough times at first but later we became inseparable." I said

"Everyone has some rough times but can you tell me what exactly was the matter between you two, if it was anything huge"

"Yeah, it is of significance but it got sorted. We both were only children. But then she had to share her mother with me."

I think he recognised that things were getting too real and intense for me because he changed the subject for good.

"I see, did you take your meds and your meals on time"?

"I did" I sighed. It felt good knowing someone was concerned with me eating but I really hated taking pills.

"What is wrong beta?"

"I don't like to take meds, it makes me sleepy" I complaint

"I see, we can reduce your dosage now that you seem to be getting better, you will be less sleepy that way."

"Really?" I asked in excitement

I was really happy about it. I had talked about this with the doc before many times she never really talked about reducing my meds ever

"Yes beta, is there anything else that bothering you?"

"Umm yeah kinda, I just had a question"

"What is it?"

"Will I have to take these meds forever? I feel like I am an ill person. I get it that this all is to help me but this feels like a temporary betterment and not permanent. I don't wanna be dependent on these pills."

"To give you a short answer. No, you don't have to take these pills forever. I understand how you feel because of these pills. Just like therapists, the pills they give you are also just to make things easier for you, it will always be you who has to do the things."

"Thank you, this makes me feel better" I smiled.

He always reassures me and makes me feel better. That's why it's so easy to talk to him. He hasn't judged me or gotten irritated by my questions.

"Mention not kiddo, I will let you read this beauty now and see you tomorrow, okay?" he said handing me the book

"Okay," I said with a smile

He left but he gave me something to hold onto. It made me wonder how everyone in my life has given me so much to hold onto. I held my mum's necklace and felt a lot of emotions rushing through me yet felt at peace. I took my meds had a proper meal even at night and slept.

THIRTEEN

Ex

"Hello Aarohi, how are we feeling today?" He said with enthusiasm

"Good, how are you?" I asked with concern

"I am doing good too but we are here to talk about you," he said with a smile

I just nodded indicating a yes.

"Did you read-

"Yes I did, I read the whole book. It's so amazing. I can relate to it a lot." I said in excitement.

"I see, why do you think you can relate so much?" he asked with concern

He was always so concerned about me and cared for me. He was like a father figure to me. If my dad were alive he would be like him or so I think.

"It's because of a guy I knew"

"A friend?"

"Boyfriend"

I don't remember when was the last time I thought about him. But he surely had an impact on me and my life.

"Would you like to talk about it"?

"Yeah, We never really met in person at first, it started when I randomly found him in my mutuals and sent him a friend request. He accepted it and we started talking. We were friends for a year or so but then we started to talk daily. We used to almost share every little thing about our day with each other. After a while it didn't feel like we were just friends, it had to be something more special, that only we shared. One day he just randomly said that he loved me. That scared me so much."

"Scared? Why do you think it scared you?"

"I always wanted to be loved and to love but I was afraid of what would happen if they left or were taken away from me."

"Has that happened with you before?"

"Yes"

"Okay, would you like to tell me more about what happened next?"

"Sure, I knew I felt something about him, I knew he was special to me. I knew he was much more than just a friend and after keeping him waiting for like a week I finally replied by saying that I loved him too. He was so happy, he was so relieved. We started dating after that. We used to meet at times. It wasn't easy but he used to travel for me. He did a lot of things for me and I won't say he didn't love me but we used to fight a lot, he always had a problem with my friends, not only guys but also girls. He wanted to control my life, he wanted me to do everything according to him. We used to talk when he felt like it. He used to leave me on read if he wasn't ready to talk about things. He used to know that I was crying but still it wouldn't matter to him. He knew I was suffering but he just didn't care. I was too in love with him to care. He used to mess up and apologise and I used to forgive him and the cycle kept going on repeat.

This was my first ever relationship and I wanted it to be my last. I knew at some points that it was wrong that I was being treated like shit. I knew it was wrong but I still couldn't let go. One day I decided to go meet him and put in a little effort from my side. And when I got to his hostel I found him kissing another girl." I said with tears in my eyes.

"It's okay my child. It's his loss, he lost such a wonderful person from his life, who truly loved him. You deserve someone who loves you, the way you love them." he said patting my head

"He always messed up like this. Why else did he let me go when I ran away? I was so naive. How could I be so naive? It was all so obvious. He never let me visit him. He always hid his friends from me. I still feel like I was responsible for it. I wasn't enough and that's why he cheated on me. Maybe I couldn't be there for him enough or maybe I didn't love him enough. I was just letting him treat me like shit because I think I deserved it. I still don't know how I deserve to be treated." I said crying.

"It wasn't your fault he cheated on you. You could have done everything enough and more but he would still act the same way. Relationships don't work in one-way beta, they work from both sides. There are many reasons why people cheat on people and the most common ones are comment issues, the need for variety, unmet needs and situations. People like you deserve to be treated with care and love, always remember that." he said with a smile.

"Thank you, it felt good after talking about it." I said smiling with tears in my eyes.

"I am glad you felt comfortable enough to talk about it."

"I always feel comfortable with you." I said as I wiped away my tears.

He smiled at me and patted my hand with love and warmth. He then asked me if I had taken my meds and eaten properly. I replied yes with enthusiasm as if i was a child getting chocolate after eatingmy veggies. He left bidding me bye and left me with my thoughts.

I loved talking to him and to my surprise I realised how better and normal it felt talking to to him about things so complicated and ugly. He never made me feel juged or pathetic. He was always so gentle and honest and things. I loved how he never forgot ask me about my meals and was so involved in just a few days. He was feeling so close to him. He was definetly going to be someone I could talk to about anything.

FOURTEEN

THE PAST

"Hello Aarohi"

"Hello Dr"

"How are you feeling today?"

"I feel better than before, lighter I think"

"Did you take your meds and had your lunch?"

"Yes, doc I did"

"That's good, can you tell me something?"

"Yes, sure"

"Why did you think you deserve to be treated badly?"

"I guess it has something to do with my childhood. I was grown without parents, I had my aunt who cared for me and loved me like my mother but she could just never fill that void you know. She did everything she could and didn't let me feel like I was missing out on anything but then I still remember my parents and that void I feel within me is just very visible. I tried to make her my everything and it worked, she surely is my everything but I still cannot forget my parents. I feel so bad, I don't act the right way even with the ones who do me good. Everything bad has happened to the ones who loved me. I feel like I am bad luck."

"Aarohi, firstly you need to understand that you can never forget your parents. It's not a void, it's just their space and you are constantly trying to fill that. Just because that person isn't in your life anymore doesn't mean you necessarily need to forget them. You can still cherish those memories which you will always carry with you. Instead of trying to forget them and calling their space a void, let them have a place in your heart that they deserve. And I hope you understand you are not bad luck. Myra, Vihaan and your aunt all of them are so happy because of you, they care about you so much and so do I."

"Yeah, I understand that," I said with a hesitant smile. "But I feel like I am troubling them, especially because of therapy, I wasn't even getting better instead I just got worse."

"Well let me tell you this, therapy isn't causing them trouble rather it means you are growing out of trouble and you are gonna be better soon I know that for a fact."

"If you are saying this then it must be true" I said smiling hesitantly again.

"You don't seem fully convinced"

"No, I am not. My aunt stopped her therapy for me and I keep feeling guilty, I know I shouldn't feel guilty and I should work on being better. But I keep feeling like I am neglecting her sacrifice whenever I don't feel the guilt."

I just said things, I didn't intend to say them they just came to me and I was thinking out loud. I felt comfortable enough with Dr to do so.

"I see. May I ask you what and why did that exactly happen?"

"Yeah. My aunt was divorcing uncle Ashwin. She was my mother's best friend in college. Mum told me they drifted apart but still managed to stay in touch somehow but once she stopped working they both lost touch. She loved her husband even tho it wasn't a love marriage. He didn't want to marry her from the beginning but still, he was very gentle and polite as if he had accepted her as his but after they had Myra he started being distant and he used to talk shit to her, tho he was good to Myra and loved her from the bottom of his heart. So she accepted him just the way he was, she cared for him and loved him. But one day he crossed his limits by slapping their 10year old for taking his phone without his permission. She thought she knew him but she didn't he cheated on her with his colleague. When she found out about it. She decided to divorce him and finally found the courage to face him and tell him to divorce her. She then called my mum immediately. It had been 11 years since their marriage and Myra was 10 years old. Aunt needed therapy but she realised I needed it too so she gave it up for me."

"I see but I don't see why she had to give her therapy up. Is there more to the story?"

"Yes yes, there is more. But she should have gotten therapy and she didn't because of me"

"Has she taken therapy later?"

"No she still hasn't and I hate that exactly. As I didn't get better it was hard to get therapy for both of us"

"Don't worry Aarohi, I will talk to her and make sure she gets the required therapy"

"What? Are you serious?"

"Yes I am"

"I cannot let you do that"

"This is my job kid, I have to do this. Don't worry your aunt is strong she will be better soon"

"I can never thank you enough"

"You can, just by letting go of the guilt you felt, as because of you she is going to get therapy okay?"

"Yes DR," I said with tears rolling down my cheeks

"It's okay beta, everything is fine"

"You made it fine DR" I said smiling with tears in my eyes.

That day I called Myra and told her to bring Aunt, Vihaan with her when she came to visit me. I broke the news to them very excitedly and happily. I told aunt to talk to DR later about this. She seemed happy but hesitant. I don't know how she was feeling but I know for a fact I was very happy for her. She was finally going to get what she needed and deserved. I was happy because I wasn't an obstacle in her therapy anymore. I looked and Myra and Vihaan and they seemed happy and excited too.

I held my aunt's hand and told her that it was time for her to do this for herself. She said she will do it and we all were very content and giggled happily together after a long time and to me, it seemed like forever.

FIFTEEN

ALONE

"Hello Aarohi"

"Hey Dr," I said a little distracted.

"Why do you seem distracted Aarohi?"

"It's 25 August tomorrow," I said looking away and zoning out.

I thought about it for a while and then I realised how my childhood defined everything for me. And how much there was which Dr didn't know. Was it because of that, that he was so sweet and caring? Because he had no idea about who I am. Will he hate me after he finds out everything? Will he refuse not only for my treatment but also aunt's? I cannot let that happen. I shouldn't say anything. I cannot stop imagining everything that happened that day I don't- I just don't want to think about it.

"I don't wanna think about it" I screamed and had a panic attack.

"Aarohi what did I tell you about the water and breathing? Follow it please."

"Yes Dr" I said trying to breathe slow.

He handed me the water bottle near me and asked me to drink the water slowly while he kept saying very reassuring things

"Beta, I am here and everything is gonna be fine. You are gonna be fine. You are doing so much better than before. I am proud of you. I know you are a very strong girl. We are going to talk about what's bothering you so it helps me, help you heal faster"

"Thank you Dr" I said calming down. Looking aside I completely zoned out.

I suddenly said

"It was my parent's anniversary that day. It was a strange day from the beginning. It was as if I was losing everything at once. Everything was falling apart little by little and then all at once.

I was out playing with my friends and my dog who was a part of our family for 5years. He died because of a car accident. He died in front of me. I couldn't save him. It still haunts me sometimes. I loved him. I loved him so much but I lost him that day. Just like that, he was just gone forever. I was just 10 years old and I witnessed my first pet's death. It was devastating. I stopped and stood there in shock looking at Leo's dead body bleeding, crushed and ruined, completely useless. I held him in my arms and because of that, I was completely covered in blood. I rushed home with his body in my hands, screaming. I went into my parent's room and my mom followed me as I was screaming so loudly. I still remember her face, how horrified she was looking at Leo dead in my hands, That's when I figured it out that he was really gone. My mom was devastated, she loved animals. But who knew something more horrible was yet to happen."

This time there was no panic just numbness. I didn't know how to express my emotions. I felt so many of them that it almost felt like I had none. I stared into oblivion. It felt like ages passed away at the same time it felt like time wasn't passing by. I realised where I was. I looked at Dr only to see him looking at me with concern.

"Aarohi are you okay?"

"No, I am not"

"It's okay Aarohi everything is fine. You are safe and loved."

"Can I be alone, please?" I said looking away

"Sure, just don't forget to take your pills and eat properly" he said patting my shoulder and left.

I felt like I was naked but wasn't being judged. I couldn't deal with the fact that I was about to talk about something so horrible. But I trust Dr Vaze, he has been nothing but sweet and kind to me. Then I don't understand why I asked to be alone. Maybe because I just don't trust anyone enough with this.

SIXTEEN

THE DAY - AUGUST 25, 2000

Later Dr talked with my aunt to gain more information about 25\8\2000

"Hello, good evening and thank you for meeting me" said Dr

"Oh, Dr no it's alright why did you ask me to meet you? Is Aarohi okay?" Aunt asked with concern

"Yes, she is fine. I just wanted to ask you what 25\8\2000 represents for you" he asked simply

"Oh right" Aunt was shocked yet came back to reality instantly.

"That's the day they were killed" she said like it didn't mean anything, looking straight into his eyes.

"I see. You are talking about her parents right?"

"Yeah and Purab too"

"Sorry, who is Purab?"

"The one who killed her parents"

"Wait WHAT"

"Yeah he died in a car accident, he was drunk and driving"

"Was he related to you all in any way?"

"In any way? Huh, I wish he wasn't but he was related to us in many ways" she said laughing sarcastically

"What does that mean?"

"He was in the same college as me and Isha. He proposed to her during our college days, she rejected him as he never stayed loyal to any girl he dated. He use to make it hard for both of us to exist in college as he was a senior but because Isha was smart we always got out of his dirty little traps. After a while, he stopped troubling us and everything went back to normal. But then she married his cousin. And he was no one else but Vihaan's Father." she said and started breathing heavily.

"I am sorry to hear this. But I am happy to see you trying to move on from all that so gracefully."

"Thank you for providing me, therapy it is helpful. Aarohi gets upset from the 25th of August to the 5th of September. It's her Birthday on the 5th. She usually hides away from all of us. We let her have her space for 10 days. After which she acts normal."

"Thank you for meeting me and sharing such intimate and valuable information. This was very helpful"

Aunt rushed to meet me. As she came in she saw Myra and Vihaan already standing beside me, trying to get my attention. I was like a corpse. I didn't move a bit. I was not doing it on purpose. I was trying to focus on what they were saying but all I could do was hear my thoughts roaring. They left after what seemed like forever. While leaving anut patted my shoulder and said "Dr is gonna help you, my child, you will be fine soon. You don't have to suffer anymore"

Later I saw someone come in and leave something on the table beside me and left immediately.

SEVENTEEN

THE BETTER VERSION OF ME

I woke up and found an envelope beside me. On the envelope was written.

Open me on 5th September

- Yours truly,

Dr Vaze

I was intrigued and I wanted to open it immediately but then I realised now I had a reason to hold onto till the 5th. I tried and convinced myself not to destroy it nor open it until the 5th. I sat on my bed staring at the wall. I took my pills on time but only ate once a day, as Dr made sure of that personally. It was amusing how much he cared for me. I didn't know I could be so loved and cared for by my therapist. He wasn't just my therapist to me, he was a father figure to me. These days were cursed. I didn't say a word to anyone and everyone around me respected that.

I don't know what use to happen to me. But I use to feel as tho everything was happening all over again. I was aware that nothing was happening but the things I felt those days was unexplainable. How scared I was, how sad and numb I was all at the same time kept coming back to me. Every day was the same I woke up, sat and stared at the walls almost all day long. I ate once and I took my meds twice per day. Slept at night and the cycle repeated.

This was a different morning altogether I knew it was near but I had no idea how near. I woke up and was staring at the walls but they were decorated already. Big balloons and ribbons were all over the room. I looked for people but there were none. I was happy and sad about it at the same time. I knew it was today and then I realised how I can finally read what was in that envelope. Excited I got up and looked at the table picked up the envelope and opened it. There was a poem and a small note.

The note read

I know life wasn't fair to you but always remember this everytime you
want to know that I am here by your side.

"I know Your Nights are Dark and Light Seems Far,
You had Your Own Battles and that's what caused those Scars!
But that doesn't mean that you gave up and kneeled,
It means that you fought, you survived and you healed!
Remember when it's Dark, stars still shine,
And wounds do Heal, may they be Yours Or Mine!
If stars don't burn, who will show the path to the Lost?
They still shine bright, even at their own Cost!
I am sure it will be fine, forever, no pain lasts,
As you have made your way through everything,
Trust me, this too shall pass!"

This poem felt like a big warm hug which I needed badly. He didn't know what exactly was going on with me but yet he was so kind and gentle with me. He was genuinely there and trying to help me feel better he didn't once make me feel judged nor did he ever make me feel uncomfortable. I couldn't stop my tears and they kept rolling down my cheeks for a while.

I know for a fact what needs to be done. I got up. Wiped my tears away and went straight to the bathroom. I looked into the mirror and felt a different version of myself staring back at me. Who was more grown and mature, I knew for sure. I knew all I had to do now was to listen to the new version of myself and everything would be just fine. And she had already told me to do a few things and I was onto them. I got ready and tidied up my room. Took my meds and waited for Dr to show up with food. As always he was on time and when he saw me he was shocked yet a smile rushed on his face. He came inside in rush and wished me.

"Happiest Birthday beta!" he almost screamed with excitement.

"Thank you so much, not only for wishing me but giving me the bestest gift ever" I said with a genuine smile

"How are you feeling now?"

"I am feeling much better Dr thank you so much."

"I am glad to hear this, come on now eat this and I will see you tomorrow"

"Dr, I got your gift but I wanna give you a return gift" I waited for a moment as I let the new version of myself take over

He looked at me puzzled but gave me a moment As he sat on his chair.

"I went through some real depression, anxiety and stuff, it kills you. It never lets you think straight, it makes you cry even when you don't want to. it makes you push people away from you, it makes you do things you never wanted to do. You become a slave of it. It has a very good and firm hold of you. It never fails to show you how shitty person you are and how bad you are for others. How you shouldn't exist. It fills you up with guilt, for literally no reason. It kills you daily. You fall apart so many times, in so many ways that you never realize when you lost yourself. It eats you up, keeps you up all day and night. It makes you hate yourself. It makes you wanna kill yourself. It makes you question your entire existence. It kills you until, you break yourself completely until, you lose yourself completely. It leaves you with your suicidal thoughts and fills you up with emptiness, with the want to hurt yourself and then with the guilt of hurting yourself. Which makes it a need to hurt yourself even more, which just keeps growing knowing no bounds and it eventually leads you to commit suicide but I am still alive. Even when I know how it is to be this broken, this hurt, I am still alive, I may not be myself right now but I am still alive and that is enough for now, only if it was enough that time. Being half alive and half dead is no fun, being angry without any reason is not cool and being sad for literally no reason, is not okay. No matter what the person is going to say they need love, care, affection and attention may it be from within or from outside, they need it. Everyone deserves to have inner peace, everyone deserves to go to sleep hoping to wake up tomorrow and everyone deserves to be loved by themselves and not have these doubts. It sucks as nothing sucked before. It breaks you to such an extent that you don't even feel broken anymore. You get comfortable living in the misery you created for yourself. Not knowing your reality is the worst, feeling worthless all the time hurts, feeling like an outsider with everyone you know hurts, believing you deserve to be mistreated hurts, and not knowing your worth hurts, it all hurts so much that you wanna let it go, you want to make it stop. End it forever and it makes you do anything for it,

anything and everything!"

I took a deep breath cause what I was about to do was above my limits but I knew for a fact I could do it. I loved the confidence I had in myself.

"Right after I went into the room I heard a voice “ISHA” screamed someone from the front door.

My mom gasped as if she knew who it was. She was scared to death and made me go under the bed and covered me immediately with the bedsheet. She knew who it was, it was my uncle. Purab uncle.

He rushed in and started screaming at my mother, he was drunk ”What do you think huh! You can reject me and marry my brother?” he pushed her to the wall and her head hit the wall making a big bang, she gasped and said “I didn’t know he was your brother, Purab” she pleaded.

Purab uncle had a knife in his hand seeing that my mother screamed at the top of her lungs, my dad came out of the bathroom rushing and he tried to save her and got himself stabbed. Purab uncle killed him in front of my eyes. I saw my father being killed and I could do nothing. I couldn’t even move or make any noise because if I did I knew I would be dead too. My mom was screaming in the background. I felt her heart stop beating. My uncle killed her too. I saw her body drop down to the floor. I remember him dropping the knife, rushing out and driving away. I couldn’t stop my tears, my whole body was numb, I didn’t make a sound, more like I couldn’t. I wanted to scream, I wanted to cry so much, I wanted to have someone by my side. But all I had around me were dead bodies. I lost everyone I loved. Everyone I cared for.

I wanted to scream knowing my parents were gone forever and ever, I didn’t want to accept the fact that I was never gonna see them again. Never. We use this word so easily and never mean it but this was a real never. This never meant forever. It was not gonna change even when I wanted it to. I wanted to end it, I wanted to die. I felt like I was supposed to die. I wanted to kill myself and what was I? Just a 13year old who lost everyone from her family. Who lost her everything. What scared me more was that I had nowhere to go and I didn't know what I was supposed to do. Luckily that was the day when Aunt and Myra came home. My aunt is the reason I am still alive, that I am still breathing. She was going through some rough time herself, she had her story to write but she took mine and intervened with hers. Even when all I ever was is a burden to her. It took me time to trust my aunt, so I tried escaping, I tried running away which made it worst. So I tried killing myself and ending it but my aunt always found a way to stop me. Later I gave in and decided to give this life a chance but so much in me was changed. No one understood why.

I was too soaked in pain. I was used to it. It felt like home. But now it doesn't. It doesn't feel like it. I don't think this is it. I wanna change this. I wanna be better I wanna talk about my pain and help others. I read your poem and it got engraved onto my soul. I can never let go of those words and the motivation and inspiration they carried. Nothing and no one has ever made me feel so understood yet telling me to move on." I finally stopped talking.

There was silence in the room. Dr was looking at me, he got up came close to me and patted my back with so much love and care. I couldn't control it anymore and started crying very badly.

"Beta, I hope you understand you couldn't have done anything differently. You are a very strong woman. You got out of such a difficult situation so efficiently. I am very proud of you. You don't realise how big of a deal it is. Never blame yourself for anything my child. You aren't responsible for any of that" he said as he held my hand in his hands.

It felt so good to finally have that masculine energy around me. His touch made me feel safe. I was thankful to speak out my worst, as he was my best. He has helped me find this mature and grown version of myself. I can never thank him enough for that.

"Can I hug you?" I asked him crying.

"We will have to call someone in, hold on"

He called out for someone and I knew I couldn't wait anymore. And I hugged him. He hugged me back. And I swear to god, ***I never felt so vulnerable yet so secure.***

A Letter For You

Dear Readers,

I know that there are times when giving up seems the best option but trust me, it's not. Trying and holding onto hope is the key. I understand that things haven't been how you want them to be and that sometimes you feel like giving up but trust me it gets better, even if you don't think so right now. One day you will be proud of yourself for going through it all and for being nothing but stronger. Remember having a fear of falling is never the problem but not wanting to get up is. So have faith within yourself and believe in yourself, that you can soldier through it cause I believe in you! Sending every one of you an abundance of love, power, strength and hope.

Yours Lovingly,

Shreya S

Important

Never hesitate to seek help. A psychologist is like google maps, they are there just to help and guide you the rest is always in your hands. A psychologist will never do 100% work for you. Therapy isn't a lifetime thing, after a while, you learn how to do better. Therapy\counselling is to help you grow, it is to help you become independent.

9 798888 150931

Printed by Libri Plureos GmbH in Hamburg,
Germany